KU-054-509

ELMER'S SPECIAL DAY

David McKee

Andersen Press

Elmer, the patchwork elephant, looked at the other elephants, and smiled. It was almost Elmer's Day – the day when once a year all elephants decorate themselves and parade. The elephants had only just begun to prepare for it, but they were already excited and noisy.

"I say, Elmer," remarked Lion. "That's a bit of a racket your chaps are making!"

"I'm sorry," said Elmer, "but the preparations are as much fun as the parade itself."

"Only for elephants," said Tiger. "Be a good fellow and quieten them down."

"Please," said the monkeys.

A little later on, the other animals asked, "How about less noise from your friends, Elmer?"
"Please," said the rabbits.

Elmer went back to the
elephants. "The neighbours are complaining
about the noise," he said. "Let's be a bit quieter."
"Of course, Elmer." "Sorry, Elmer." "Certainly, Elmer."
"Right ho, Elmer." "Don't worry, Elmer." "We'll be
quieter than quiet, Elmer," the elephants promised.

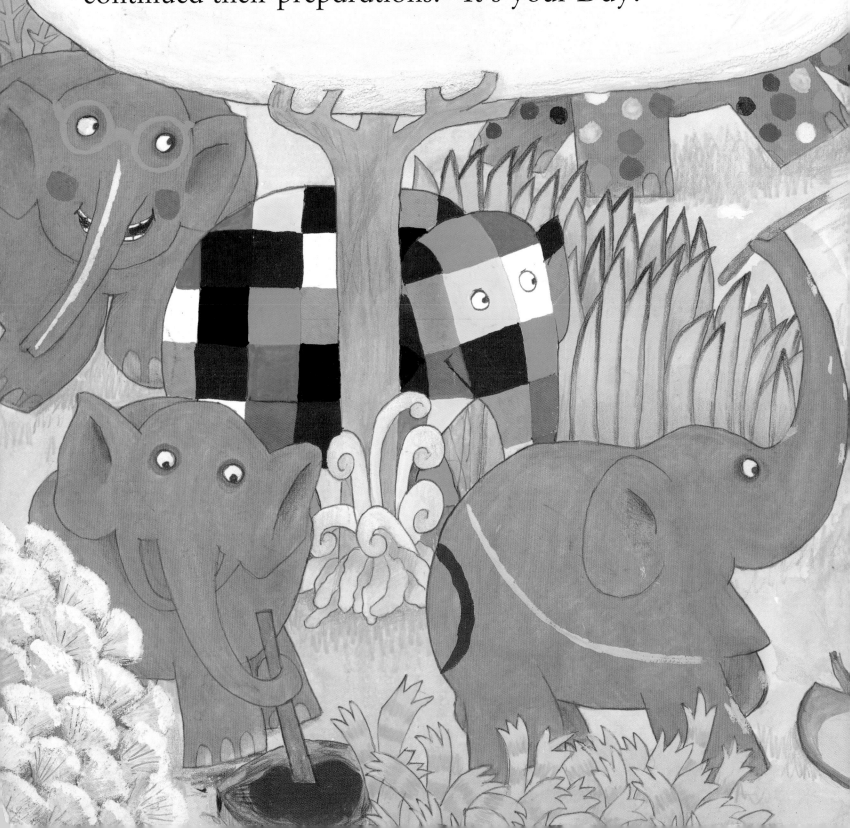

But ten minutes later the elephants were noisier than ever!
"Listen," said Elmer, "I've an idea."
"Whatever you like, Elmer," said the elephants, as they
continued their preparations. "It's your Day!"

Elmer returned to the other animals.
"I'm sorry about the noise," he said. "But this year is a
special year, because you are all invited to join the parade.
Of course you will have to decorate yourselves."
The animals were really excited.

Gradually every corner of the jungle became filled with the sound of laughter and preparations for the parade. "What a racket!" thought Elmer looking at the elephants. "And what a mess! I wonder how the others are getting on?"

The other animals were just as messy
and noisy as the elephants. Elmer chuckled.
"Well at least no one is complaining now," he
thought. "Do you mind, Elmer," said Bird. "We'd
rather you didn't spy on our preparations!"

At last the big day came. The tradition was that on Elmer's Day only Elmer could be elephant-coloured, so, as usual, Elmer went to the bush with the elephant-coloured berries and covered himself with berry juice until he looked just like an ordinary elephant. Then he returned to the herd.

The other elephants were ready and waiting.
"The parade can begin as soon as the other animals
arrive," said Elmer. "Listen! Here they come!"

The elephants stared in amazement as the animals arrived.
Then they cheered. "Wonderful! Fantastic!" they shouted.
Not only were the animals decorated, but they all wore
elephant masks.
"You see, it's still an elephant parade!" Lion laughed.

"Let's begin," called Elmer from the front of the parade. "From now on everyone can join in the Elmer's Day Parade . . .

...as long as they wear an elephant mask!
This will be the best elephant parade ever!"

"And everyone," said Elmer, "means everyone!"

Read more ELMER stories

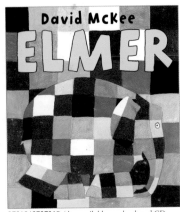

9781842707319 Also available as a book and CD

9781842707500 Also available as a book and CD

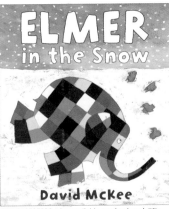

9781842707838 Also available as a book and CD

9781842709504 Also available as a book and CD

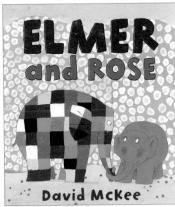

9781842707401

9781842708385 Also available as a book and CD

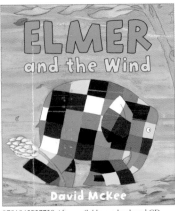

9781842707739 Also available as a book and CD

9781842707494 Also available as a book and CD

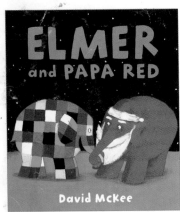

9781849392433

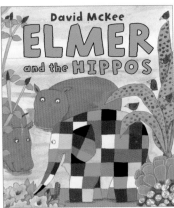

9781842709818

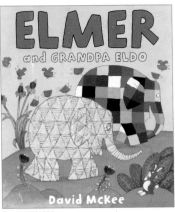

9781842708392

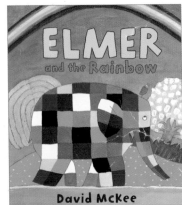

9781842707166

Find out more about David McKee and Elmer, visit:

www.andersenpress.co.uk/elmer

Especially for my Bakhtina

LONDON BOROUGH OF WANDSWORTH	
9030 00001 9757 2	
Askews & Holts	10-Nov-2011
JF CY MACK	£5.99
	WWX0008409/0027

This paperback edition published in 2011 by Andersen Press Ltd.
First published in Great Britain in 2009 by Andersen Press Ltd.,
20 Vauxhall Bridge Road, London SW1V 2SA.
Published in Australia by Random House Australia Pty.,
Level 3, 100 Pacific Highway, North Sydney, NSW 2060.
Text and Illustration copyright © David McKee, 2009.
The rights of David McKee to be identified as the author and illustrator
of this work have been asserted by him in accordance with
the Copyright, Designs and Patents Act, 1988.
All rights reserved.
Colour separated in Switzerland by Photolitho AG, Zürich.
Printed and bound in Singapore by Tien Wah Press.

10   9   8   7   6   5   4   3   2   1

British Library Cataloguing in Publication Data available.
ISBN 978 1 84270 985 6
This book has been printed on acid-free paper

This ELMER book belongs to:

· ·

9030 00001 9757 2